RAINBOW RIDGE ELEMENTARY SCHOOL
15950 INDIAN AVE
MORENO VALLEY CA

D0435849

DATE DUE		

1040006566

F
CLI

Clifford, Eth.

Harvey's mystifying
raccoon mix-up

RAINBOW RIDGE ELEM SCHOOL
15950 INDIAN AVE MORENO VLY CA

867379 01271 37890A 38240E   006

Harvey's Mystifying Raccoon Mix-Up

Also by Eth Clifford

The Dastardly Murder of Dirty Pete
Flatfoot Fox and the Case of the Missing Eye
Flatfoot Fox and the Case of the Missing Whoooo
Flatfoot Fox and the Case of the Nosy Otter
Harvey's Horrible Snake Disaster
Harvey's Marvelous Monkey Mystery
Harvey's Wacky Parrot Adventure
Help! I'm a Prisoner in the Library
I Hate Your Guts, Ben Brooster
I Never Wanted to Be Famous
Just Tell Me When We're Dead!
The Man Who Sang in the Dark
Never Hit a Ghost with a Baseball Bat
The Remembering Box
The Rocking Chair Rebellion
Scared Silly
The Summer of the Dancing Horse
Will Somebody Please Marry My Sister?

Harvey's Mystifying Raccoon Mix-Up

Eth Clifford

Houghton Mifflin Company
Boston

Text copyright © 1994 by Eth Clifford Rosenberg

All rights reserved. For information about permission to
reproduce selections from this book, write to Permissions,
Houghton Mifflin Company, 215 Park Avenue South,
New York, New York 10003.

Library of Congress Cataloging-in-Publication Data

Clifford, Eth, 1915-
  Harvey's mystifying raccoon mix-up / by Eth Clifford.
    p.   cm.
  Summary: Twelve-year-old Harvey and his bossy cousin Nora get
involved with counterfeiters, imposters, and a pet raccoon when they
find a prowler outside the house one night.
   ISBN 0-395-68714-4
  [1. Mystery and detective stories. 2. Counterfeits and
counterfeiting—Fiction. 3. Cousins—Fiction. 4. Raccoons—
Fiction.]   I. Title.
PZ7.C62214Hat 1994   93-27471
[Fic]—dc20   CIP
              AC

Printed in the United States of America
BP 10 9 8 7 6 5 4 3 2

This book, with love, is for my Canadian family:
Rudy, Ze'ev, Shira and Shimon in North York
and for Alan in Winnipeg

Contents

Contents

Harvey's Mystifying Raccoon Mix-Up

1

In which a
sinister shadow appears

"*Pssssst.*"

A snake had just hissed in my ear. I tried to scream but couldn't because a giant hand had clamped my mouth shut. My heart thudded loud enough to wake the dead.

"*Harvey.*"

I knew that voice. It belonged to my cousin Nora. I opened my eyes and glared at her. I couldn't speak because her hand was still pressed so hard against my lips, they felt as if they had been glued shut. I tried to shove her away, but Nora shook her head. Then I realized she had a wild look in her eyes. Nora was scared.

My stomach began to churn. I'd seen that

look in Nora's eyes before. Disaster, I told myself.

"Harvey," she said finally, "listen. Don't try to talk. Just listen."

This time I managed to push her hand away. I sat up in bed, ready to tell her what I thought of someone who sneaked into your room when you were asleep and then hissed in your ear. But I was stopped cold by what she said next.

"Harvey, somebody is sneaking around under your window." She took a deep breath before she added, "And he has a *gun*."

I stared at her, then glanced at the clock. It was five A.M! In the morning! On spring vacation!

"Are you crazy?" I was spitting mad, but I kept my voice low. I sure didn't want to wake my mom and dad, especially my dad, who has a short fuse and a temper to match. "Just because you had a nightmare, you came in and woke me up? Go back to bed, Nora."

She didn't move, just folded her arms and gave me a stony look. Her eyes seemed larger than usual in her owl face, larger and terrified.

Nora is the champion liar of the world, as I discovered when she visited us before. But now I finally believed her. She was truly afraid.

When I didn't seem to react fast enough, she insisted, "Why don't you go see for yourself?"

I didn't really want to look, but I had to make sure she was telling the truth.

Nora jumped off my bed, tiptoed to the window, and put her fingers to her lips to caution me. The window was open, and as usual, a large branch of the tree that was too close to the house had begun to rest on the sill. My mom and dad fight about that tree. Mom wants it cut down. Dad says he loves that old tree; he used to climb it when he was a boy. Mom was willing to compromise. "Then cut down that branch. Some day during a storm it will crash right into Harvey's window."

Dad agreed to that, but somehow never got around to it.

So, because the branch was in the way,

Nora peeked out one side of the window, and I peered down from the other.

She gave a strangled gasp. "Harvey, he's still there. Look."

Now I saw a shadow that seemed to appear and disappear. Then the shadow moved away from the huge oak into a patch of pale moonlight. No wonder whoever lurked down below seemed to be no more than a shadow: From head to foot, the figure was clothed in black. A black ski hat covered his head. Black gloves hid his hands. That was scary enough, but what made both of us catch our breath was the way moonlight gleamed on the long barrel of a rifle.

He seemed to have his gaze fixed on my window. Then I realized he was concentrating on something in the tree.

When I had gone to bed, a slight breeze had rustled the leaves, a sound that always helps me fall asleep. Now the breeze had grown stronger, and the branch began to tremble.

I studied the street as far as I could see.

No one was out—not a solitary person any-where.

"Not a living soul is out there," Nora whispered. "Except him."

Of course the street was deserted. At five A.M., why wouldn't it be? There were porch lights on here and there, but mostly the houses were dark and silent. It seemed everybody in the whole world was sensibly asleep, except for Nora, me, and the sinister shadow below.

"What do you suppose he wants? What's he looking for? And why does he need a gun?" Nora whispered.

She sounded as if she expected me to know all the answers, now that I'm twelve. I couldn't respond, though my mind twisted and turned over this puzzle. I was busy with my own silent questions.

Why would anyone want to hide in the dark like that?

Why aim at *my* window?

Whom, or what, was he aiming at?

Nora had begun to shiver. The wind had grown stronger.

"It's him. He must be a witch or something . . ."

"A warlock," I said. "A witch is a lady. A man is a warlock."

Nora glared at me.

My mom understands, though. When I learn something new, I always have to share it, whether anybody else is interested or not.

I don't know what Nora was prepared to say, because at that very moment, the figure lifted the rifle. And aimed it directly at us.

"Duck!" I told her, and yanked her down to the floor. We felt too paralyzed to move any further.

We just held our breath, and waited for the sound of a shot.

2

In which
bedlam breaks loose

A moment passed, then two, then three. Had the prowler changed his mind? Well, I sure wasn't going to peer out again to see. Nora sat up with her arms clutched against her shoulders. The breeze was working on becoming a chill wind now. I wanted to reach up and slam the window shut, but I wasn't about to become a target.

Nora slid back down to the floor and began to crawl away.

"What are you doing?" I wanted to know.

"I'm going to get Uncle Thor." She kept her voice so low I could hardly hear her. "He's a judge. He'll know what to do."

"My dad isn't that kind of judge," I reminded her, though of course she already knew he's a traffic court judge and doesn't hear criminal cases.

"I know that." She was impatient. "What's important is who he knows, not what he does."

"Who he knows?" I repeated. "Oh." You know how in cartoons, when a character gets an idea, a little light comes on over his head? If I had looked up just then, I would have seen one of those lights shoot off a brilliant glow.

"Oaty Clark," I said. "The police chief."

Nora looked smug.

That made me simmer. After all, I had been exploded out of a deep sleep and handed the bad news while I battled to get my eyes open. Listen, who thinks at five A.M.? Sometimes my brain doesn't get started until way after breakfast.

Naturally I sounded irritated when I said, "I don't have to get my dad. I can call the police myself."

"But your dad can get the *chief*," she pointed out.

She was right, another reason why it's hard to like her. People who are right all the time are hard to live with, and that's the honest truth.

"Okay," I said. "You still want to go get him?"

Nora bit her lip. "I don't think Uncle Thor will believe me," she admitted after a moment.

I had to swallow a grin. Of course he wouldn't. Who would, when everyone knows she is an all-out liar?

I stood up, well away from the window, and took one last look, just to be sure the prowler was still there. He had lowered his rifle, probably because the wind had begun to shake that loose branch wildly.

"I think he's changed his mind," I whispered. I spoke too soon, because that was when bedlam broke loose. With one swift movement, the prowler raised his rifle, aimed, and fired.

The first bullet hit the branch just where it had been working loose from the tree. I heard a sharp crack, and then that branch sailed downward and right through my open window, just as Mom always said it would. I hit the floor seconds before the branch fell, and sent Nora sprawling just as she had begun to stand up. The second bullet broke the upper panes of the top window. Shards of glass showered over and all around us.

"He's trying to *kill* us." Nora sounded jittery and furious at the same time.

I couldn't believe it.

"*Why?*" I was just as angry as Nora. "Why would he want to kill us? We don't even know who he is or what he wants. We don't even know what he looks like, with that dumb ski hat pulled down over his face."

"We're kids!" Nora was outraged. "Why would anybody want to shoot kids?"

Before I could think of an answer, the door swung open and my mom and dad spilled into the room. Mom held one hand against her chest, as if to control the pounding of her heart. Dad's hair practically stood on end. His face was so pale it looked chalky.

When Mom took in the branch and the broken glass, I could almost see the words "I told you so" tremble on her lips. I must admit that the branch looked bigger on the floor than it had on the tree.

Dad got right to the heart of the matter. "We heard shots."

Mom moved her hand up to her throat, the way she usually did when she was very upset. "They sounded like real bullets."

The only bullets my mom has ever heard have been on TV shows, but I knew what she meant. Once you hear them, you're not likely ever to forget that sound.

"All right," Dad said. "What's been happening here?"

"There was this shadow under the tree," Nora began. "I saw him and came and woke up Harvey."

I nodded. "I saw him, too. He had a rifle . . ."

Dad interrupted. His face had gone from chalky white to red. That meant his temper had started to boil.

"You saw a prowler lurking outside? With a rifle? And you woke Harvey? *Harvey?*"

"I didn't want to disturb you, Uncle Thor," Nora began.

"She didn't want to disturb me," Dad repeated. He glanced up at the ceiling and shook his head in disbelief.

"Just look at this room," Mom wailed. I think she wanted to distract him, but it didn't work. He just kicked shards of glass out of the way, shoved the branch to one side, and strode to the window, all the while muttering under his breath.

"Dad," I cautioned, "he could still be out there."

"Nonsense," he said. "He'll be long gone by now, whoever he is."

My dad was right, of course.

The man with the rifle had disappeared.

3

In which a
branch comes alive

While Dad was at the window, Mom gave
me a disapproving look. "You should have
called us right away. Your father knows how
to handle situations like this."

Nora and I exchanged glances. I could almost hear what she was thinking. My dad
knows how to handle situations like this? I
know my dad. He would have raced down
the steps, rushed outside, and tried to cap-
ture the prowler, rifle or no rifle. When my
dad gets mad, he doesn't always think first
and act later. He's a big man, but he would
have been no match for a man with a gun
who didn't mind using it. The prowler
would have shot my dad down in cold blood.

"We were so scared, we couldn't think

straight," Nora explained. My mom nodded, and sighed.

"I understand," she said. Then she studied my room and sighed again. "Just look at
this mess."

My dad had come away from the window.

"I'm calling Oaty Clark," he said.

"Let's get the room cleaned up first,"
Mom objected. "Harvey can't go back to
sleep with his room in this condition."

I couldn't believe she said that—go back
to sleep after I'd been scared out of a year's
growth?

"Absolutely not," Dad told her. "I don't
want anything touched. I have to get some
snaps of the room first."

My dad is a camera buff. He'll take a picture of anything that catches his eye—a dog
asleep in a patch of sunlight, a cat yearning
after a bird in a tree, a fly on a pie. The
subject matter isn't important, he says, just
what you bring of your own imagination and
skill to it. I have to admit he is really very
good at what he does.

He tore out of the room, and was back
with his camera before we even had time to

sort out our thoughts. He stood on a chair; he stretched out on the floor. He did all but stand on his head. Finally he said, "I'm calling Oaty now. Don't anybody touch a thing in here."

When he left the room, Mom said, "As long as we're all up, I might as well make breakfast."

The minute she was gone, I told Nora to leave so I could get dressed, but before she could do so, we were both stopped cold.

The branch had begun to quiver.

Neither of us could move. I felt rooted to the floor. I'm sure Nora did, too. She licked her lips as if her mouth had gone dry.

I forced myself to back away.

"Let's get out of here," I whispered. "That branch is *alive.*"

You think you would have been braver? Maybe so, but when a branch comes to life all by itself, I want to be someplace else.

All of a sudden a dark, furry shape rocketed by so fast it must have set a world record.

Nora made a small sound, as if the breath had been knocked out of her. I flattened myself against the wall. You think that's not a normal reaction? What would you have done?

Take my cousin Nora. She is not normal. While I tried to figure out how to levitate myself out of the room, she whizzed past me. In seconds, she held a quivering, terrified animal in her arms. She made small, quiet sounds to soothe it while she ran a gentle hand over its body. When she turned toward me, her smile was like a beacon.

"Harvey, look at this beautiful animal," she crooned. "You're beautiful, do you know that?" she asked the creature.

The animal seemed to agree with her. He snuggled down in the safety of Nora's arms, relaxed by the singsong of her voice. Then he began to examine us with curiosity.

His fur was kind of a mixed gray, brown and black. The most remarkable feature was his face. A black mask around the eyes gave him an especially appealing look.

Nora's eyes shone with joy. "It's a raccoon. A beautiful, beautiful raccoon."

Well, he was hard to resist, but if you

know Nora the way I do, you'd realize she would consider a hippopotamus or a giant sloth beautiful, too.

Just then my mom yelled up the stairs. "Are you two coming down sometime today? What's keeping you?"

I watched the way Nora floated out of the room, the raccoon peaceful and content in her arms. I dressed quickly, then followed her, deep in thought.

I knew exactly what would happen, because I recognized that look in Nora's eyes. Her idea of a perfect world is one in which there are only animals, with a few people here and there to love them to pieces.

"Nora," I warned. "Don't start getting attached to it."

"Me? Don't be silly, Harvey. I'll put him outside the minute we're in the kitchen."

That was a laugh. Put that creature outside? *Nora?* She would as soon part with her right arm.

When we walked into the kitchen, Mom spun around to ask how we wanted our eggs, spotted the raccoon, and exclaimed, "What

in the world?" She would have added to that
if the doorbell hadn't interrupted her.

"That can't be Oaty Clark." Mom was
surprised. "Your father is still on the
phone."

Just then my dad came in. "I'll get the
door," he told us. His jaw dropped when he
saw our next-door neighbor, Mrs. Motley,
with her finger glued to the bell. He was as
surprised as we were, because Mrs. Motley
is kind of a night owl, and sleeps quite late
in the morning.

Mrs. Motley is a tiny lady, with wispy gray
hair and bright brown button eyes. She looks
gentle and meek, but she's like a tiger when
she's all riled up. She has an expression for
it, "don't get my Irish up," which is funny,
because she isn't Irish at all. She is a born
and bred native of Liverpool, England.

"It's only me, love," she told my dad.

Dad didn't blink an eye when she called
him love. She calls everybody love.

"I thought I heard shots," she explained.
"It didn't sound like the telly."

She didn't wait to be invited; just walked
to the table and settled in comfortably.

"I could do with a cuppa," she told my mom.

A cuppa is her way of asking for tea; she drinks it so strong a spoon can stand up in it all by itself.

Mom put up the tea kettle while I tried to fill Mrs. Motley in on what happened, with a lot of interruptions from Nora.

"You shouldn't have left your house," my mom scolded her. "Especially when you heard shots."

Mrs. Motley shook her head. "My neighbors are in trouble, and me hide safe behind a locked door? No, love, that's not the way I'm built."

While we'd all been busy talking, Nora had hidden the raccoon low in her lap; no one had paid any attention. Suddenly, though, my dad and Mrs. Motley became aware of the animal.

"What in the world?" my dad yelled.

The raccoon, who seemed quite curious now that he was calm, struggled up from Nora's lap and wiggled his way to her shoulder, where he draped himself like a scarf around her neck.

"Where did that animal come from?" My dad wanted to know—and he wanted to know this very minute.

Nora explained quickly. Before anyone else could speak, Mrs. Motley asked, "Are you going to keep him, child?"

"Oh, yes," Nora said.

"Absolutely not." My mom can take animals or leave them alone. It's different with our dog, Butch. He's been with us forever, so he's a member of the family. Right now he's at the vet's, because his breathing has become labored. He's so old, we don't take any chances.

"Now, Nora," my dad said, in what he thought was a reasonable voice, though he had begun to boom.

"Oh please," Nora pleaded. "He won't be any trouble at all, I promise. Please let me keep him."

Mom hesitated, then glanced at my dad. I could see the word NO tremble on his lips. Nora saw it, too, and she looked so crushed and miserable, my parents couldn't stand it.

"For a little while," my dad gave in. "But

only until we find out if it's someone's pet, understood?"

Nora nodded joyfully.

"But only," my mother put in with great haste, "if you promise that the animal won't be any trouble."

"I give you my word," Nora said, her eyes solemn. "You won't have a minute's trouble with him. I promise."

It's a good thing, I suppose, that we can't any of us look into the future, because, the truth is, that appealing little animal turned out to be TROUBLE in capital letters! But Nora insisted, naturally, that what took place in the days to come was not his fault.

4

In which a
bullet is found

The next time the doorbell rang, we knew
who it was. Only Oaty Clark puts his finger
on a bell and keeps it there until you open
the door. The police chief isn't a patient
man. He's the only person I know who can
make a chime sound like an alarm.

Let me tell you something else about
him. Oaty Clark looks like a strung-out
beanpole, with hair that appears to be bor-
rowed from a scarecrow. It's wispy and
shoots out from his scalp in all directions.
His small brown eyes are practically hidden
behind scrunched-up eyelids, as if he's
standing in strong sunlight and can't keep
his eyes open. His long, narrow head sits on
a long, skinny neck. And in that neck a big

Adam's apple bobs up and down when he talks. He may not win prizes for looks, but my dad says Oaty Clark has a mind like a steel trap.

When my dad let him in, Oaty Clark was all business. He wanted Nora and me to explain—one at a time, he said—and he glared at us. Well, it wasn't my fault that Nora interrupted me all the time. When we stopped talking, Oaty Clark said, "I need to inspect the bedroom."

Naturally, we all trailed him upstairs and watched him closely while he studied my room.

Nora was having a wonderful time now. She whispered to me, her eyes bright with excitement, "If there was a body on the floor, he'd have to outline it with chalk."

"Great," I snapped back. "That's all I need up here, after being shot at. A body on the floor."

I wished she hadn't put that image in my mind. How did she expect me to be able to sleep in my room ever again?

Oaty Clark looked around. "Harvey, you

said the first bullet hit the branch and broke it off."

Mom gave my dad a knowing look. "I knew that branch would crash into Harvey's window some day."

My dad didn't remind her it took a bullet to do it, just wondered aloud where the second bullet could be. Wouldn't you know it would be Nora who spotted it first, in the ceiling over my bed.

My dad went and got a ladder from the hall storage closet, then wanted to scramble up it, but Oaty Clark stopped him. "Just hold it steady for me, Thor," he said. The chief dug the bullet out with a pocket knife. He sure was thoughtful as he tossed that bullet up and down in his hand.

My mom pressed her lips together real hard. She glanced up at the hole in the wall over my bed and shuddered.

"What kind of a madman goes around trying to shoot children?" she whispered.

"We don't know for sure that's what he was doing," Oaty Clark said, trying to comfort her.

When my mom gave him a furious look, my dad leaped in with the usual solution.

"Let's go down and have breakfast," he decided. "We can't solve anything standing here."

So we all trooped downstairs again, and while Mom began to beat some eggs, Dad got the coffee going.

Oaty Clark, between bites of a cinnamon roll, continued to concentrate on the prowler. "Harvey," he began, and he seemed to pin me down with his eyes. I sure wouldn't want to be a suspect he was grilling. "Harvey, are you sure you can't describe him at all?"

"He was all covered up," I repeated. How many times was I going to have to say this?

"Just take your time," he insisted. "Go back in your mind and try to visualize that prowler. He was a shadow moving in shadows . . ."

"And he had a rifle," Nora said.

I ignored her. "He was all covered up . . ." I didn't realize I had said the words aloud. "He was almost invisible. Then the moon shone on the rifle. He moved. His shadow lengthened . . ."

"He was tall," I said. I felt triumphant. "His shadow was long. Tall and thin."

Oaty Clark gave me a triumphant smile. "Good boy, Harvey. Solid thinking."

"That's right," Nora said. "Harvey is right."

Oaty Clark beamed at both of us.

Nora was puzzled. "But how does that help?" She wanted to know.

"Obviously I'm just grasping at straws," Oaty Clark said. "Right now, any little bit of information is something to file away in my mind for later."

He turned to Mrs. Motley.

"I understand you're somewhat of a night owl. You would have spotted someone running or walking fast, especially if he had a rifle. That would have attracted your attention."

"No, love," she said. She sounded regretful. "I didn't see a living soul. Except that nurse person, of course."

"Oh?" Oaty Clark put down his coffee cup. He stared at Mrs. Motley intently.

Mom shook her head, but before she could say a word, Mrs. Motley leaped in. She liked the center of the stage and she wasn't going to give up a chance to shine. "That nurse can't be your prowler. Sure she's usually out late at night, but she's always pushing poor old Mrs. Grandy in her wheelchair. She can't walk, you know. Not the nurse. Mrs. Grandy."

My dad began to get restless. Mrs. Motley rushed on. "Poor old thing suffers from insomnia, you know. Guess getting out at night relaxes her, like sitting on my porch relaxes me. Not sociable at all, though. Never talks to anybody."

"And you never see one without the other?"

Mrs. Motley shrugged. "Well, I'm not out on my porch every single night, love, am I then? The funny thing is, though, I've never seen them outside in the daytime. You think old Mrs. Grandy is allergic to daylight?"

"How can you be allergic to daylight?" Nora wondered.

"You can be allergic to anything," I told her. "Well, you can, you know," I added, when she stared at me as if I had informed her that Martians had just landed in our back yard.

"That must be it," my mom put in. "When they first rented the house about two months ago, I went there to welcome them to the neighborhood. But there was a big sign on the door: Do Not Disturb. The bell was hanging loose, disconnected. All the shades were down to the sills. And there wasn't a sound from the house."

"Hmmmmm," said Oaty Clark. "No deliveries, either?"

"Oh yes, love." Mrs. Motley kept a close watch on what went on in our block. "Not often, mind you. A few packages now and then. Not that it's any of my business, mind. Folks that want to keep themselves to themselves—I don't pry."

My mom and dad exchanged amused glances. We don't need a local paper on our block—Mrs. Motley keeps well informed, and doesn't mind sharing tidbits about the neighbors.

"I see," Oaty Clark said, but it didn't seem to me he did, because he had a puz-

zled frown that cut deep between his eye-
brows.

Oaty Clark shook his head, took a fast
swipe at the eggs which had grown cold on
his plate, drained his coffee cup, and stood
up, ready to leave. "Well, there's nothing
else I can do here for the moment. I'll be in
touch, Thor."

When the door closed behind him, Dad
stood up, too. "I might as well shower and
shave." He was halfway up the steps when
he turned around and came back.

"Harvey, I want you and Nora to clean
up that mess in your room. And be extra
careful getting all that glass up off the floor."

"I can take care of that," Mom offered,
but Dad shook his head.

"Absolutely not, Joy. The kids are young
and strong and capable. And the mess is in
Harvey's room."

Is that fair? I had nothing to do with what
happened in my room. Why should I have
to clean it up? I began to argue, but stopped
when I saw the expression in my dad's eyes.

Mrs. Motley made a halfhearted attempt
to leave, though it didn't take much to per-

suade her to stay for another cuppa. She lives alone. That's hard on a person who is not only talkative but extremely curious as well.

Nora went to get a trash can. The raccoon unfurled himself from around her shoulder, scooted down her arm and popped into the can. Mom and Mrs. Motley and Nora all laughed. I thought it was kind of dumb. When Nora scooped him up again, she told the raccoon how clever he was. He made a cheerful chirping sound in agreement.

"Cute as a button, that one is." Mrs. Motley's head bobbed up and down.

Nora beamed, like a mother receiving a compliment on her newborn baby. She squeezed the raccoon, who didn't seem to mind one little bit.

"That's exactly what you are, cute as a button." Her eyes shone with delight as she turned to my mom and announced, "That's what I'm going to call him, Aunt Joy. Buttons."

Mom sort of bit down on her lower lip, a habit she has when she's worried. "Now, Nora," she began.

"Buttons, Buttons," Nora cooed.

The raccoon nuzzled her as if the name sounded just right.

Mom plunged on. "Nora, I don't think it's a good idea to give him a name. He's not a pet, understand? He's a creature of the wild, and that's where he belongs."

"I know," Nora agreed at once. "It's just for now, Aunt Joy. But I can't just call him hey-you. He has to have a name meanwhile."

Personally I think animals should have sensible names, like my dog Butch. But then Nora is a girl. Girls think names have to be cute.

To tell you the truth, though, I didn't really care, because there was no way she could keep him. What could she do, take him on the plane with her when she flew home? Present him to her mother, my aunt Mildred, who would faint dead away the minute she laid eyes on him?

Mrs. Motley stood up. "Well, I'll be running off then." She kind of inched her way to the door, still reluctant to leave. She started to go out, then turned back. Her eyes seemed to glaze over, as if she was looking inward. "Listen, love," she told my mom. "We haven't heard the end of this matter. Mark my words."

After she left, Mom looked unhappy. Nora's eyes began to glint with mischief. She said in a spooky voice, "We haven't heard the end of this."

She was right, of course. I just hate it when she's right.

5

In which a
mirror reveals a secret

I decided we should get rid of the window
glass first. It was tricky, for while the large
pieces were easy to grasp, the tiny shards,
with their sharp edges, were a problem. You
wouldn't think a window had so much glass.
It felt like forever before we were done.

While we toiled, Buttons sat on my bed
and watched us with interest. Nora worked
hard, but she couldn't resist stopping now
and then to coo at him. If an animal can
beam with pleasure, that's how Buttons reacted. I have to admit—a raccoon can get to
you. I already had a fondness for him,
though I'd never let Nora know. Then I
thought about Butch. Was I betraying him
by liking another animal? No. Butch would

understand. After all, he's been my dog forever.

When we were finished with our task, Nora wanted to know, "What will we do about the branch? It's too big to break up."

Ha! So much for girls being smarter than boys. I gave her a superior look, hauled the branch to the open window, then tugged at it until it was up on the sill. After that, it was a cinch to push it out.

Nora looked down. "Uncle Thor isn't going to like the lawn messed up like that, Harvey."

I knew that, didn't I? What Nora didn't realize is that we have this machine that grinds up branches. In our house, we recycle everything.

While we peered at the lawn, Buttons leaped off the bed. When we turned around, we couldn't believe our eyes. Buttons held something in his hands. I know, I know— they aren't hands. But he used his paws just like human hands.

"What's he got?" I asked. "Where did it come from?"

I moved closer. To protect his find, Buttons fled under my bed. From there, he made some defiant sounds, as if to warn me he'd found this treasure, and it was his. I swear if that animal could talk, he would have told me, "Finders, keepers."

I tried to reach him but he just retreated farther back.

"Listen, Nora. Help me push my bed against that far wall. Then we can grab him when he runs out."

"No, Harvey. You'll scare him. Why can't he keep whatever it is?"

I had an answer for that. If it wasn't mine, and this was my room, where did whatever it was come from? And how come Buttons spotted it, and we didn't?

Too many questions popped in and out of my mind to be ignored. So I began to push and tug my bed. After a minute, Nora helped, though she was still reluctant about it. Of course Buttons raced out. He practically climbed her like a tree to get to the safety of her arms.

She clucked and soothed and stroked until Buttons calmed down. How she persuaded him to let go even one edge of his treasure, I'll never know. While he still clutched it with one paw, she grabbed the other end. It was a piece of metal, no larger than a dollar bill.

"Harvey, look. It has some sort of printing on it."

I moved closer to examine it. Buttons let out a shrill cry that set my teeth on edge.

Nora immediately sprang to his defense. "Don't upset him, Harvey. Buttons is very sensitive."

He was sensitive? After what I had been through this morning, somebody should have been worrying about me.

"Do you think you can get it away from him? Without breaking his heart, of course, so I can get a good look at it?" I said.

"Do you have something shiny you can let him have to take its place? Maybe he won't mind if it's an even exchange."

The word tumbled round and round in my head. Shiny. Shiny. What did I have that was shiny? Then I had a brainstorm. I ran into my sister Georgeann's room and came back with a brass buckle she changes from belt to belt. It was almost the same size and shape as the whatever object Buttons refused to part with. My sister loves that buckle because her forever boyfriend Hank Clay gave it to her. If somebody gave prizes for ugly, that belt buckle would win top honors.

"That was clever, Harvey."

It was a good thing Georgeann was away on a camping trip. She'd kill me if she ever found out. Buttons was torn between grabbing the buckle and releasing his treasure. Finally, shiny won out. He seized the buckle and leaped onto my bed, where he chirped at his new toy.

Now that I had the object in my hand, I was still puzzled. What was it? Where had it come from? What did one do with it?

We had no idea.

"What's all this stuff that looks like printing?" Nora wanted to know.

I shook my head. "I can't make it out," I admitted.

Then something happened. Remember I mentioned how light bulbs click on in cartoons when characters have an idea? Well, one clicked on over my head just then so brilliant it should have blinded Nora.

"Watch this, Nora."

I gave her a triumphant smile. I'd show her who was smart when it really counted. I walked to the mirror over my dresser. When I held it up, we could read the words clearly.

FEDERAL RESERVE NOTE

was printed in block letters across the top. Under those three words, in a kind of ribbon effect, it said:

UNITED STATES THE OF AMERICA

On each side of the scroll design was the same number: 20. The center featured the picture of a man who didn't look especially pleased to be there. At first, the name under the picture, in fine print, was hard to read.

Nora squinched her eyes so that just a narrow space remained for her to peer through.

"Jackson," she said, and looked thoughtful. "Who's he?"

So much for girls being smarter than boys. "He was a president," I told her. "Everybody knows that."

"I'm only eleven," she shot back at me. "I don't have to know the names of all the presidents until . . ." she hesitated, then took a wild guess, "until I'm twelve."

"You'll be twelve in three months." I would have said more but just then my door swung open. My dad popped in to check out the room. He was pleased to see what a good clean-up job we had done; but then he noticed my bed had been moved.

"Harvey Willson, why is your bed over there?" he demanded.

If there is one thing my dad absolutely cannot abide, it's furniture out of place. Every once in a while, my mom gets bored and rearranges the living room. When Dad comes home, it sounds like World War III. Mom fights a good battle, though she always winds up moving everything back. She can't stand it when Dad is unhappy, mostly because he's unhappy at the top of his lungs.

Nora tried to come to my rescue.

"We had to move the bed, Uncle Thor,

because Buttons found something. See? Show him, Harvey."

Dad winced when she said Buttons. He doesn't appreciate cute names any more than I do. That didn't stop him from taking whatever it was from my hands. He examined it, slow and easy, with a deep frown.

"Dad," I said. "It's a reverse twenty-dollar bill. I bet it's funny money."

I thought it was phony money, like you use in some games.

"It's funny money, all right. This is a printing plate. A real old-fashioned printing plate. For turning out counterfeit twenty-dollar bills."

"Why is it old-fashioned?" Nora wanted to know.

"Counterfeiters use much more sophisticated methods these days." Dad frowned, pursed his lips, then asked a question I couldn't answer.

"Where did this come from, Harvey? How did you get this?"

"It was Buttons," Nora admitted. "He found it when we moved the branch."

As if Buttons knew he was in deep trouble, he snuggled down as far as he could into Nora's arms. Of course, she held him in protective custody. Even if Buttons had done something wrong, no one, not even my dad, would be allowed to harm him. He looked so appealing I had to grin. I must say those bright, black eyes surrounded by the black mask got to me, too.

So I came to his defense. "It wasn't his fault, Dad. I guess he was just curious. He seems to like shiny things."

"Maybe that's what the prowler was after. The plate," Nora said. "Maybe he's the counterfeiter."

"Good thinking, Nora." My dad gave her an approving smile.

Nora flashed me a triumphant look. She was so pleased with herself I could hardly stand it.

"And it wasn't us he shot at. It was Buttons. He didn't find the plate here. He must have had it when he ran up the tree and along the branch that almost hit my window. That prowler wanted to get Buttons," I said.

"You've hit it right on the nose," Dad said. After a moment, he added thought-fully, "At least we've solved that mystery."

He tossed the plate back and forth, then went on, "Oaty Clark has to be informed about this."

I thought that meant he would be off to the phone at once. I should have known bet-ter. He put the plate on my night table.

"First things first, Harvey. Your bed goes back *now*."

When my dad says *now* in that voice, he doesn't mean a little bit later, or when you can get to it. Now means *now*.

So Dad and I pushed my bed back in place. It looked better there, naturally. I guess I'm a lot like my dad. If something is right, leave it alone.

Nora put Buttons down so she could straighten out the sheet and plump up the pillow. Fuss, fuss, fuss. Why do girls do that?

Dad brushed his hands together, some-thing he does when he's real pleased. Then he turned to pick up the printing plate from the night table. But it was gone.

Buttons had reclaimed his property and left the buckle in its place. When Dad yelled at him to drop the plate, he gave Dad a startled look, scooted out the door, and fled. A pack of baying dogs couldn't have made him move any faster.

We rushed after him, pell-mell, down the steps, through the hall, and into the kitchen. I noticed out the corner of my eye that someone else was now in the kitchen with my mom and Mrs. Motley. It was that nurse person. I didn't have time to wonder why she was there because I was concentrating on Buttons.

So was everyone else.

"Pickled horse feathers," Mrs. Motley exclaimed. "If that doesn't beat a band of monkeys!"

She wasn't the only surprised person in the room. We were all stunned.

With the printing plate held in a firm grip in one paw, Buttons calmly stood up, stretched to reach the doorknob, turned it, pulled the door ajar, and slipped through.

"Stop!" Dad shouted.

It was too late.

6

In which
Nora takes a tumble

Of course we all made a mad dash after him.

The nurse spotted him first. "Look," she shouted. "There he is. Way up there, in the tree. And he's got the printing plate in his mouth."

She was right. With the plate secure in his mouth, Buttons had already made his way up to the highest branch. He scooted along it to our house, then squeezed himself through a space under the eaves into the attic.

"Don't yell," Nora told the nurse. "You'll scare him."

"If I get my hands on that miserable little thief," Dad exploded, "he'll be more than scared. That plate has to go to the FBI."

I guess the look Nora gave my dad then, one of pure horror, reminded him how Nora feels about animals.

"Now, Nora, you know I won't harm him. I realize he doesn't know what he's doing. But I must get that plate."

Without another word, Dad dashed back to the house; we all trooped after him. Now I know how people feel who hunt—something about a chase makes the blood rush through your veins.

I don't know if any of our neighbors saw us. If so, it must have looked odd—Dad and Mom, Mrs. Motley, the nurse, Nora, and me. Now that I thought about it, I wondered what that nurse wanted. She'd never come to our house before.

The nurse must have caught my glance, because she explained at once. "I came to ask about the shots. So scary, you know. And I stayed to make sure no one hurts that poor dear little animal."

Another Nora, I decided, and promptly caught up with the others. By the time I was back in the house, my dad was well up the steps to the attic.

He muttered under his breath as he struggled with the key in the lock. It had rusted somewhat, for it hadn't been used in a long time, and it is somewhat damp up there.

"Why do we keep this door locked, Joy?" Dad asked in frustration.

I knew why. It was habit. You see a key in a door, you turn it. After all, that's why it's there in the first place. Right?

Dad was just about to kick the door in when the key turned.

Once inside, Dad had to search for the cord that hung down from a clear bulb in the ceiling. It helped a little, but it also cast a lot of shadows. I was glad I wasn't up here alone. An attic can be scary, and the shadows didn't help.

"This place looks like Frankenstein's cellar," Mrs. Motley whispered, as if the monster might pop out at us without warning. "All the junk in the world must be up here. No reflection on you, love," she apologized to my mom. "That's why we have attics, you know."

"I'll be glad to help you look for that

plate," the nurse offered. "You'll never find it alone."

"I want to find Buttons first," Nora insisted. First things first with her. She didn't care about the plate. But suppose Buttons was still frightened?

As if he recognized her voice, Buttons made a sudden appearance. He had the plate in his mouth.

"GRAB HIM!" Dad shouted. "STOP!"

My dad expects everyone to pay attention when he raises his voice. Of course, Buttons didn't know that. He did what any sensible raccoon might do: He escaped out the same opening through which he had entered. Buttons had to leap up on some boxes to do so, but that didn't hold him back.

"Wait," the nurse shouted. She almost sounded like my dad then, harsh and angry. "He's still got that plate in his mouth."

I was puzzled. Why was she so upset? Why did it bother her? I wondered if she was a retired FBI agent. Once an FBI agent, always an FBI agent, I figured.

My dad came to a sudden decision. "Harvey, you and Nora stay up here. I'm going down to stand under the tree. The animal will be scooting down. When he sees me, he'll probably race back up here."

"I could climb up those boxes and grab him when he comes back," I said.

"Make sure you get that plate away from him, Harvey," Dad told me. "And be careful. Those boxes aren't stacked too securely."

"I'd better be the one to climb up the boxes and wait for Buttons," Nora said. "Because he'll come to me."

I didn't like it, but she was right. Buttons would probably turn tail and escape if he saw me.

"I just hope that animal hasn't come down already and gone into hiding somewhere," my dad muttered as he left.

"Wait," the nurse called after him. "I'll help you catch him."

I never saw anyone leave a room as quickly as she did.

"Isn't she nice?" Nora said with appreciation. "I guess when you're a nurse, you care about everybody, even animals."

Mom had been moving about restlessly. Now she said, "I don't see how I can help. I'm sure you two can handle the raccoon. Just don't scare him. He is a wild animal," she cautioned. "He could bite if he feels cornered."

"Listen to your mum," Mrs. Motley chimed in. "A cornered animal can turn on you like *that*." She snapped her fingers sharply.

"Mrs. Motley and I are going back to the kitchen," Mom said.

They had no sooner left the attic when we heard Buttons. I helped Nora climb up on the boxes. They seemed a little shaky but Nora got to the top without a problem. Just as she stopped climbing, Buttons scooted in, the plate still held securely in his mouth.

Nora made a sudden lunge at him; the boxes shifted and toppled over. Nora came sprawling down and Buttons tumbled head over heels to the floor. While Nora and I sorted ourselves out, Buttons did an instant disappearing act.

My dad raced in, with the nurse right behind him, took in what had happened, and scowled at me. I thought he was about to give me what-for for my clumsiness. Instead he sighed, shook his head, glanced at his watch, then ran his hand through his hair.

"I can't pursue this any further," he said reluctantly. "I'm due in court. I'm depending on you, Harvey, and you, Nora, to make a thorough search of the attic. Find Buttons. If you can't find him, find that plate. With the boxes down, he can't reach that opening now. There's no way he can run off with the plate now."

The nurse seemed about to speak, but my dad just went on politely, "Thank you for your help. After you," he added, and pointed to the door.

For a minute, I thought she was going to protest, but I guess it was just my imagination, because she said, "Do let me know if you have any luck finding the plate. It's been a most exciting morning."

She went through the doorway with my dad right behind her.

Suddenly, the attic seemed too quiet. I

knew my mom and Mrs. Motley were down in the kitchen, but right now they seemed miles away.

"We'd better get started, Nora," I said. I figured the sooner we began, the quicker we could leave.

When I spoke my voice echoed in the empty space, even though I had kept it low. Have you ever noticed how, when you're in a scary situation, you either scream your head off or talk in a strangled whisper?

Nora glanced around the attic. "Where? Why did your parents buy a house with such a big attic?"

"They didn't know you'd adopt a raccoon or they wouldn't have had an attic at all." I was sorry the minute the words left my mouth. Nora had every right to feel over-whelmed. To search up here for something the size of a dollar bill would be like a life sentence.

When Nora didn't answer, I moved closer. Her eyes had grown larger and glazed over. When she spoke, her voice was flat, the words drawn out, as if she were under a spell.

"There is danger in this place, Harvey. Evil lurks here."

Naturally I got a creepy-crawly sensation that someone had just come up behind me. I spun around fast. But whichever way I turned, whatever it was whirled with me. I knew it was all in my mind. It didn't help. So I did the only sensible thing I could think of; I got real mad at Nora.

"If you don't cut out your doomsday speeches, I'm leaving, no matter what my dad does to me later!"

Nora reacted the way I expected she would.

"Okay. I won't do that anymore." Then, as if she couldn't help herself, she added, "But remember my words."

"I'll remember, I'll remember. So can we get to work now?"

Talk, talk, talk. What could happen in an ordinary, everyday normal attic?

7

In which Buttons
plays hide-and-seek

I have to tell you—I don't like attics and basements. When I grow up, my house will be all on one level. Maybe I feel this way because Georgeann scared me in both places when I was real little. She thought it was fun to jump out from behind things and scream *Booo!* She grew out of that kid stuff later on, but I don't think I ever did. I have a complex about it, I guess. I read that someplace. It means you're scarred for the rest of your life.

When I mentioned that to Georgeann, she shook her head in disbelief.

She said, "You always were chicken."

"Better a live chicken than a dead duck," I replied.

My dad thought that was funny. I don't
know why.

So you can understand, me with that fear
from my early childhood, why I was uneasy
in the attic now. Of course I wasn't alone,
but tell me honestly, if you were in an attic
with a cousin like Nora, would you be relaxed?

Nora began to poke around the boxes that
had fallen.

"Nora," I said, "you think Buttons would
hang around those boxes after they scared
him?"

"You're right," she agreed.

That was a surprise.

She looked around, and I could see she
felt as helpless as I did.

"Where do we start?" she asked.

I shrugged. "Why don't you call him? He
seems to trust you."

She brightened at that. "Buttons," she
cooed. "Here, Buttons."

Wherever he was, Buttons wasn't falling
for that sugary note in her voice.

Not knowing what else to do, I began to

pull drawers open in an old chest. Nora shook her head.

"You expect to find Buttons in one of those drawers?" she wanted to know.

"Maybe Buttons put the plate in here. It's as good a place as any for hiding things," I told her. Well, at least I was trying.

Without warning, Nora froze and gazed upward. I looked up, too. Had she spotted Buttons? After a minute or so, I grew restless.

"What is it? Do you see him? I don't see him moving. What's he doing?"

"Be quiet, Harvey," she told me. "I'm just trying to think what I would do if I was a raccoon."

Now I understood what Mrs. Motley meant when she said that some things get her Irish up. I decided I'd have to be methodical about this hunt—by starting at one end of the attic and working my way across. Nora could stay in her trance for all I cared.

That was when we heard him: Suddenly Buttons scooted out from behind a small trunk and headed for the door. I was happy to see he still had the plate.

Great! Our problem was solved.

"Grab him," I screamed at Nora. That was easier said than done. Do you have any idea how fast a raccoon can move when he wants to?

Buttons made a headlong dash for the door. He reached for the knob, turned it, opened the door, and fled. Of course we were after him in a flash, but by the time we came to the steps leading down, Buttons had disappeared again.

"Now what?" I asked. I have to admit my feelings about Buttons were beginning to change. I was in no mood for a chase from room to room. Our house isn't all that big, but it did provide a lot of places where a small animal could hide.

"Tell you what," I suggested. "You start looking in the rooms from that end of the hall, and I'll do the same from this end."

Nora agreed. She went off, calling in a soft voice, "Here, Buttons. Come to Nora, Buttons." I didn't bother calling. I started with my sister Georgeann's room, then the bathroom, and from there into my room. I pushed and pulled and poked, but Buttons was nowhere in sight.

I noticed Georgeann's buckle where Buttons had dropped it on my night table and I stuck it in my pocket. I figured when all the hullabaloo was over, I could put it back in Georgeann's room.

When I went back to the hall, I met Nora, who looked defeated.

"Maybe he went downstairs. Maybe he's in the kitchen with Aunt Joy," she suggested. "He's probably hungry by now."

That sounded reasonable to me, so we started down the steps when all of a sudden the TV set came on with a blast. Nora grinned. "I'll bet that's Buttons. I bet he turned on the TV."

I believed her. Why not? He opened doors, didn't he? I wanted to get downstairs fast, so I slid down the banister, with Nora right behind me, and rushed to the living room. Mom stood in the doorway, a startled look on her face.

"How in the world?" she began, but Nora and I just laughed.

Buttons sat on my dad's easy chair and watched TV as if he knew exactly what the program was all about. In his hand—excuse me—paw, he clutched the precious plate.

Nora cautioned me with a finger to her lips. Then she slowly sidled up to the chair. Buttons gave her a quick sidelong glance but didn't try to escape. He seemed fascinated by what was on the screen. As it happened, a leopard was stalking a fawn, and I swear you'd think Buttons was worried about the fate of the fawn. This must be the kind of thought that flashes through Nora's mind. For a minute, I almost understood her.

Mom stood frozen in the doorway, afraid any movement of hers would startle Buttons into flight again. Nora edged up to Buttons, then held out her arms.

Buttons was cagy. He shifted in the chair. He was wary of Nora, yet he couldn't seem to take his eyes off the leopard. At that moment, the leopard pounced, and so did

Nora. Before he knew what had happened, Buttons was cuddled in Nora's arms.

Mom heaved a sigh of relief, then hurried to turn off the set. The silence was beautiful.

"Get the plate away," I mouthed at Nora. She nodded, but getting the plate proved to be no cinch. Buttons resisted. I had a brilliant idea. I reached into my pocket for Georgeann's buckle, then held it up for Buttons to see. Sunlight from the window hit the buckle and made it sparkle.

Buttons gave it an interested look. Slowly, I moved closer and closer. Finally, I reached out and held the buckle within grabbing distance. Buttons dropped the plate, which Nora had the presence of mind to snatch, and I gave him the buckle.

"This is not a gift," I told him. "It's a loan, understand? If I don't return Georgeann's buckle, she will turn me inside out and skin me alive."

Buttons made some kind of a sound which I hoped meant he understood me.

"I'm phoning your father," my mom said.

"He can come home for lunch and pick up the plate then."

"He'll probably get Oaty Clark to come over, too," I said.

Mom nodded. "Thank goodness this is over and done with," she said.

I agreed it was all over and done with. I guess I never learn, do I?

8

In which Harvey's
hair stands on end

Oaty Clark was already in our kitchen when
my dad arrived. When he saw the plate in
Oaty Clark's hand, Dad heaved a sigh of
relief.

"That plate has been on my mind all
morning," Dad said. "I was tempted to
break away from court and come home . . ."

"You what?" Mom interrupted. She
couldn't believe he said that. Neither could
we. My dad is a dedicated traffic court
judge. Ask the people who've been brought
up before him.

While Dad talked, Oaty Clark concen-
trated on the printing plate. Finally he
shook his head. "Wally Wurble," he said.

"What's a Wally Wurble?" Nora wanted to know.

So did I. It sounded like something you ordered for dessert. I'll have a Wally Wurble, with whipped cream.

Oaty Clark laughed. "Not a what. A who, Nora. Wally Wurble is a counterfeiter. As a matter of fact, he was just released from prison last year."

I was curious. "How can you tell who the counterfeiter is just by looking at the plate?"

"Simple, Harvey. Wally Wurble slips up on details. That's why he's always caught. Look at this plate. What do you see?"

Near the kitchen door, Mom had put up a rack with hooks for our wet clothing in case we get caught in the rain. In the center of the rack is an oval mirror. I held the plate up to the mirror, but couldn't see anything unusual. I puzzled for a while, then had a bright idea. I ran to the desk in the living room and got a magnifier Dad uses to study some of his pictures. Now I could see what Oaty Clark had spotted. I grinned. Nora joined me, and soon she grinned, too.

"President Jackson's eyes are crossed," I said.

"And look at this." Nora pointed. "Can you read what it says?"

"Sure. It says *this note is legal tender for all bets, public and private,*" I said. "What's wrong with it?"

"It should say debts, not bets." Oaty Clark shook his head as I handed him the plate.

Buttons, who had curled up on the counter with his eyes glued hopefully on a dish of crullers just out of reach on a high shelf, turned suddenly. I guess the kitchen light was making the plate gleam. He leaped down, then up into Nora's arms, and tried to grab the plate. Georgeann's buckle lay abandoned on the counter. While I got up in a hurry and grabbed the buckle, Oaty Clark held the plate out of Buttons's reach.

"He wants the plate," Nora said. I had the feeling she'd give Buttons the moon if he had his heart set on it.

"This plate is going to the FBI," Oaty Clark said.

Mom looked at him thoughtfully. "Then it was Wally Wurble under the tree. He was trying to shoot Buttons in order to get the plate away from him."

"It had to be," my dad said, but Oaty Clark shook his head.

"Harvey," he asked me. "Describe the prowler again."

I sighed. "How can I describe someone who was practically invisible? He was just a shadow."

"But you saw moonlight reflected on his rifle." Oaty Clark sure had a great memory for details. "Think hard, Harvey. He had just stepped out where you could see him."

Then I remembered what I had already told my dad. "It was the shadow he cast. It lengthened. So I guessed he was tall. And thin."

Nora agreed. "It was a long, skinny shadow."

My mom was puzzled. "I don't see, Oaty, what you can make of all this. We still haven't any idea what that man looked like.

How can you identify anyone from his shadow?"

Oaty Clark shrugged. "At this point, I'm still grasping for straws. For example, I know from this tiny bit of information that it couldn't have been Wally Wurble."

I'm sure my jaw dropped. Oaty Clark sounded like Sherlock Holmes. Maybe that's what I would be when I was grown—a famous detective who solved unsolvable cases. "How do you know that?" I asked.

Oaty Clark shrugged. "Wally Wurble is short and heavyset."

Mom sighed. "So we're back to square one again."

"Not exactly," Oaty Clark told her. "Wally has a partner, Kookie Smith."

"Kookie?" I repeated. "You're kidding. What kind of a mother would name her baby Kookie?"

Oaty Clark grinned. "His mother named him Cliveden. Cliveden Harbison Smith. The kids in school called him Kookie."

Mom didn't look happy. "You mean we have to worry about two of them?"

Oaty Clark shook his head. "They probably realize by now this plate is a lost cause. They may just go ahead and make a new plate."

"Look at the time," Dad said then, leaping to his feet. "I've got to get back to court."

"Don't speed, Thor," Oaty Clark joked.

The day passed somehow. In between playing with Buttons and finding shiny objects for him to clutch, Nora and I tried out a Nintendo game my sister Georgeann gave me for my birthday. Mom let us grill hamburgers and franks in the back yard. We even went to the library so Nora could look up piles of information about raccoons. She also took out some ghost stories on my card and insisted on reading some real scary stuff to me when we got home. I prefer science fantasy myself: It's scary but safe. I mean, the Star Trek world isn't exactly right around the corner, is it?

I have to tell you, I was glad when bedtime finally rolled around. It had been a long hard day—the shots, the panic, wrestling with a raccoon for a counterfeit plate . . . I yawned. I was positive I'd be asleep before my head hit the pillow. But that didn't happen. My eyes were wide open, and my brain was in turmoil.

I thought about Nora. I felt really sorry for her. At least I have my dog Butch; I've had him practically forever. But Nora has never had a pet. Her mom, my Aunt Mildred, is a jumpy, nervous, twitchy lady who is scared of her own shadow. Have an animal in her house? Are you kidding?

I picked up a book to keep my mind occupied, but the words just blurred on the pages. Nature took over, finally, though; my eyelids began to droop. I was just about to turn out the light when I heard a sound directly overhead.

Someone was tiptoeing in the attic!

My hair stood on end, believe me. I took a deep breath and held it, trying to calm my nerves. My teeth were clenched so hard that my jaw ached.

I wished now that I hadn't listened to all of Nora's ghost tales, particularly those about ghosts in the attic. According to Nora, attics are a favorite hangout for them.

I forced myself to lean back against my pillow. I gave myself a good talking-to. That was Nora's problem, an overactive imagination. Not mine. Of course not mine.

Finally I reached over again to turn out the lamp on my night table. My hand froze in midair.

I had just heard that slight skittering sound again. That sound was for real.

Someone—some thing—*was* in the attic.

I didn't know what to do. Should I wake my dad? Suppose I had just imagined I heard something. Maybe it was the rising wind, and the thunder still off in the distance—the storm we had been promised would hit us late at night. Wind can produce lots of eerie sounds, and our attic wasn't airtight. My dad does not take kindly to being awakened for no good reason.

So I did the next best thing. I went to Georgeann's room, opened the door slowly, and tried to peer through the darkness at the bed.

"You can come in, Harvey," Nora said. "I'm not asleep."

She turned the bedside lamp on, and I could see how woeful she still looked.

"Nora," I said. "Don't get alarmed . . ."

So of course she became alarmed.

"Something's happened to Buttons," she cried. "He's dead, isn't he? Somebody's killed him."

I was glad I don't have Nora's imagination.

"Will you calm down a minute? Nothing's happened to Buttons. It's just that I think I heard someone walking in the attic."

Nora's hand flew to her lips.

"You think there really are ghosts in the attic?" she whispered.

"Don't you know anything at all?" I sputtered. "Ghosts don't have feet. Everybody knows that. When was the last time you saw a ghost with feet?"

We both fell silent. I listened as hard as I could. So did Nora.

"I guess whoever it is is over my room right now," I said.

So we went, silent as shadows, back along the hall to my room, where we did the same thing. We listened and listened. Nothing. Then, all of a sudden, we heard that slight, skittering sound.

"Somebody is up there," I insisted.

"Why would anyone want to go up in your attic?" Nora asked so softly you'd think whoever was upstairs would hear her if she spoke in a normal voice.

Just then there was a sudden clap of thunder. That storm was moving fast. We both jumped, though Nora pretended it hadn't bothered her at all. There was a sudden lull. Then we heard that sound in the attic again.

Nora shrugged it off. It was irritating to see how calmly she reacted to it. Then she said, "Floorboards creak, Harvey. Maybe there's some air whistling around up there, through the cracks or something."

She was so reasonable, I started to feel convinced. The truth is I wanted to be convinced.

I breathed a sigh of relief. "So you think that's all I heard, just some usual nighttime creaks?"

Then Nora had an idea. It made her eyes

light up like bright stars in a clear night sky.
"It must be Buttons."

I shook my head. Mom had put Buttons
in Butch's dog house on the back porch. Of
course, Buttons could have come in through
Butch's panel in the door, but why would
he want to? Raccoons sleep, don't they?

"Why would Buttons suddenly decide to
come into the house in the middle of the
night?" I wanted to know.

Nora glared at me. "Maybe he has insomnia."

"Raccoons do not have insomnia, Nora.
People have insomnia. You and I have insomnia right this very minute . . ."

I would have gone on, but she could have
stopped traffic with her commanding upheld
hand.

"I don't care what you say, Harvey. I'm
going up there and get him."

"Go ahead. Who's stopping you?"

She tossed her head, as if to say, "Who
cares?" She marched to the door, where she
paused uncertainly.

"What if there really are ghosts in the
attic?"

She sounded so fearful, I felt sorry for her.

"Okay," I grumbled. "But when we find Buttons, hang on to him. He's got to go back into the dog house. No more fun and games."

"I promise," she said.

So up we went on tiptoe.

And it was probably the most terrible mistake of our lives.

9

In which there is
talk about hydrophobia

We didn't have to turn on any lights. My mom is a strong believer in nightglow bulbs, most of them with pink shell covers. She doesn't like a dark house. To tell the truth, neither do I. So we were able to go up the steps very quietly.

When we came to the door, however, I stopped short. Nora was about to burst into angry speech, so I put my hand over her mouth. Then I nodded at the door. It was open just a crack. When we had left it that morning, I had closed and locked it. I motioned her to follow me down the stairway. When I thought we couldn't be overheard, I said, keeping my voice low just in case,

"Did you see that? The door was open. I locked it, remember?"

She was so anxious about Buttons, she whispered impatiently, "What's the matter with you, Harvey? You know Buttons can open a door."

I shook my head. "He's clever, Nora. But not that clever. I don't believe for a minute that he can turn a key in a rusted lock after my dad had a hard time trying that this morning."

That made her stop and think. I could tell by the way she bit her lip and stared off into space.

"What we ought to do is get my dad."

Nora didn't like that one little bit. I could tell why. She was afraid my dad would think she was too obsessed with Buttons. He might decide Buttons had to go. The mere thought of that brought tears to her eyes. She brushed them away angrily. Then what did she do? She turned on me. Can you believe it?

"You're just chicken," she said. "You're a scaredy cat. You think we're going to run into some ghosts or something. Well, you can do whatever you want, but I'm not going to leave Buttons up in the attic all by himself. Suppose he's hurt? Suppose he's sick?"

By this time, she had so convinced herself she pushed by me and went back upstairs. On tiptoe. To make sure my parents wouldn't hear her.

I stayed where I was for a moment, listening hard. Then I forced myself to move on up ahead of her. After all, I am bigger and stronger. When I was at the door, I edged it open bit by bit, afraid it would squeak. Then I pulled back so abruptly Nora ran into me.

"Don't talk," she whispered. "I don't want Buttons to get scared." Someone was already here, and it wasn't Buttons. There were two intruders, each one with a flashlight in hand. We watched in fascinated horror as the beams lit up different parts of the attic.

I don't know how long we remained frozen in place, afraid to retreat, too scared even to breathe. Now I understood why animals caught in headlights turn into statues. It's simple. Fear paralyzes the brain.

I tried to send my dad a mental picture of

the situation. It didn't work, of course. My dad is one solid sleeper.

While we were very much aware of the intruders, they hadn't noticed us . . . yet. They began to talk in low voices.

"How do you know it's still here?"

"How many times do I have to tell you? I saw the police chief come out of the house. He was shaking his head. And why was he shaking his head, dummy? Because those kids never found the plate. That's why."

I almost laughed out loud. Sure Oaty Clark was shaking his head. He still couldn't get over the cross-eyed president, and how the counterfeiter had changed the word debts to bets.

"This is stupid. It's the stupidest idea you've had yet. Look at this place. It would be easier to find a needle in a haystack. Let's get out of here," one prowler said.

"It's got to be here," the other argued.

"Well, you stay and find it. I don't like this place." A close clap of thunder made him leap in the air. "You know I'm nervous as a cat in a storm. Anyway, the thunder is bound to wake up everyone in the house. I say we go now, while the going is good."

"Okay. But if I lay my hands on that miserable animal, I'll wring his neck. That's a promise."

I hoped Nora hadn't heard that, but of course it was too much to expect. She was up in arms at once.

"No, you won't," she snapped. "I'll get the SPCA after you. I'll call the FBI."

They must have been shocked to hear her voice come at them out of the darkness—I was stunned myself. "Are you out of your mind?" I whispered. I grabbed her arm and tried to head her back toward the door, but it was too late.

They pointed their flashlights directly at us, and we were caught open-mouthed in the beams. Then they moved across fast and grabbed us before we had time to think. The silence in the way they reached us was eerie, until I noticed they had covered their shoes with heavy socks.

Both were covered head to foot in black, with ski caps pulled over their faces. Even

their hands were hidden in thin dark plastic
gloves, I guess so they wouldn't leave fin-
gerprints behind. It made them appear sinister and evil. I've seen figures like this on
TV, but take my word for it, in person it
gives your goosebumps goosebumps. They
were mean, and dangerous, and scared us
witless even before they spoke. The one
who had Nora shook her like a rag doll. He
was the shorter one of the two, and a whole
lot rounder as well. The other had an iron
grip on my arm. He was tall and bony. Even
though I couldn't see his eyes clearly, I
knew they had to be an icy green, hard as
marble, and twice as cold.

"All right," the one with Nora said. "You
kids live here. You play with that stupid animal. What did he do with it?"

He shook Nora again when she didn't answer. If he had done that to me, I probably
would have told him whatever he wanted to
hear, and a lot more he didn't. But he made
the mistake of calling Buttons stupid. She
knew he'd hurt Buttons if he could.

"How can she talk when you do that?" I
asked. It wasn't that I felt brave. It was just I

was afraid he'd shake her teeth loose, maybe even addle her brain. I didn't have to worry. Nora's brain operated real well.

When he eased off shaking her, and waited for her to speak, she raked him up and down with a scornful look.

"You must be an awfully dumb crook, to break into this house . . ."

My hand flew up to my head. I was convinced Nora would provoke them into killing us. I could just see that headline in the papers: TWO KIDS, WHO NEVER DID ANYBODY ANY HARM, FOUND IN ATTIC. Of course, we wouldn't be around to read it, thanks to Nora.

The person who held her was so startled, he almost lost his grip.

"What?" he stammered.

"Don't you know whose house this is?" she went on.

The prowlers waited to find out. So did I. What did she mean, whose house this is? As far as I knew, there was nothing special about it.

Nora plunged on. "It belongs to the judge. The *hanging* judge."

The way Nora emphasized that word, drawing it out, even got to me. Well, look at it this way. Suppose you find yourself in the hands of criminals, probably bloodthirsty, in the small hours of the night in a dark, creepy attic. Everything seems bigger than life—the shadows, the odd sounds, the menace of the two sinister strangers.

"Isn't that right, Harvey?"

I nodded, then realized they hadn't even noticed. So I echoed Nora, in as hollow a voice as I could, "The hanging judge. She's right. If you're real lucky, and go to jail instead, that judge locks you up and throws away the key. It's *life,* guys."

After a brief silence, the smaller man snarled, "Okay, you've had your fun. If there's anything I can't stand," he told his partner, "it's a couple of smart-aleck kids. You two want to see the sun come up, stop fooling around and tell us where it is."

"We would if you'd tell us what you're looking for," I said. "We can't read your minds."

The man who held me twisted my arm so hard, tears popped into my eyes.

"The printing plate, wise guy. Where did that miserable animal hide it?"

"How should I know?" I asked. When he twisted my arm again, I added quickly, "I honestly don't know."

Okay, so I cheated when I used the word honestly. Of course I knew where it was—safe and sound with Oaty Clark, if he hadn't already turned it over to the FBI.

"I'm going to find out where it is if I have to beat the truth out of you," he said. He raised his flashlight and was about to crack me over the head when Nora came to the rescue. Talk about quickness of mind—hers moves with the speed of light sometimes.

She leaned over and bit him on the hand. That's what I said, *bit* him. Hard.

He writhed with pain, dropped her arm in a hurry, and tore off his plastic glove. He turned the flashlight on his wound and said, with disbelief, "She went right through the glove. I'm *bleeding*. She drew blood."

I couldn't see his face, of course, but I felt sure he had turned green. The sight of blood, especially your own, can do that—make you sick to your stomach.

"You'll probably get hydrophobia." Nora's voice oozed sympathy. "You can die from that, you know."

"Hydrophobia," the man repeated with horror.

"Don't be stupid," his partner said without pity. "You can only get hydrophobia from an animal."

I had a quick thought. "Sure. That's true. But the raccoon bit her and he has hydrophobia. So naturally she has it now . . ."

"And I gave it to you," Nora told him. "I think you should go to a hospital right away and get your shots. That's the worst part of hydrophobia—the shots."

He stepped back as if she'd given him the plague. *"Shots?"* he repeated in a hoarse voice.

"You only get twenty-four," she explained. "Right smack in your stomach. The first week, of course."

His hand flew to his stomach. *"Twenty-four?"*

"The first week," I said.

"You feel like you want to die." Nora shuddered.

"She's right. It's a living death." I didn't know what that meant, exactly, but it sounded awful.

Nora looked startled. Well, if you embroider the truth, you might as well be fancy about it.

They left in a hurry, but not so fast that they made any noise. They wanted out, but they wanted it without getting caught.

Nora grinned at me. I shook my head and said, "You were terrific. And really brave." I didn't add that she showed more gumption than I did. It's okay to praise someone, but you don't have to overdo it, right?

I must say we both felt triumphant, until we heard the key turn in the lock. We stared at each other in shock.

We had only meant to scare them away, and we had. But as we glanced about, we had to admit—we were petrified.

10

In which a
key is turned

What happened next really surprised me. Nora burst into tears. She sobbed, "Harvey, I don't want to come to your house anymore. Too many dumb, scary things always go on around you. Why can't you be normal, like other kids? Why is everything such a big deal with you anyway?"

My jaw dropped so low, it could have scraped the floor. Me? Not normal? *Me*, Harvey Willson, the perfect victim for all her wild ideas? Just as I was about to whip back a scorching reply, she sniffed, wiped her nose with the back of her hand and apologized.

"I'm sorry, Harvey. I didn't mean that. I've just been so scared . . ."

"Listen," I told her. "We were both scared. But you were terrific."

"I was?" She sounded doubtful but happily surprised.

"All those things you told them, and biting that guy. I have to admire your guts, Nora."

If somebody had ever told me I would say such words to Nora, I would have laughed myself sick. But right is right, and fair is fair. What would I have done without her? Listen, this session we just went through with the intruders, the storm, the gloom of the attic, the weird time of night . . . I admit freely that I am not the world's bravest person.

"Let's bang on the door and scream our heads off," Nora suggested. "That will wake up Aunt Joy and Uncle Thor."

"How are they going to hear us with all this racket going on?" I wanted to know. For the storm had increased in intensity. Roll after thunderous roll seemed to concentrate right around our house. We could hear the crackle of lightning when it split the sky.

"Don't tell me they're sleeping through

this storm." Nora sounded resentful. "My mom would have had us all up and hiding in closets by now."

I believed her. And I even could understand how my Aunt Mildred felt. I am not a great admirer of thunderstorms.

To distract her, I said, "Well, at least we know who those two were."

"We do?" she asked with surprise.

I shook my head. I suppose Nora can only concentrate on one thing at a time. All she had been interested in was saving Buttons.

"Of course," I said. I know I sounded superior and I had a right to be, because I hadn't put my brain on hold, even though I was petrified with fear. "Wally Wurble and Kookie Smith. Who else knew about the plate, and who else would be so desperate to get it?"

"The man with the long, thin shadow," Nora said. "And we still never got a look at his face."

"I don't think I ever want to see his face," I said. I didn't know what he looked like, and I was sure I never wanted to find out.

Nora had begun to pound on the door.

For good measure, she also kicked it. Unfortunately, every time she did, the thunder drowned her out.

"Look," I said finally. "Let's not panic, okay? Sooner or later, the storm will pass, and then my mom and dad will surely hear us."

"I'm not staying in this attic a minute more than I have to," she told me. "So do something, Harvey. You're older than I am. I'm just a guest. You're supposed to look out for me."

That came as news to me. Still, there was a touch of truth in what she said. I looked around as I tried to come up with an idea. As usual, she beat me to the punch.

"Maybe we can push the key out of the lock from this side," Nora suggested.

"And then what?" I wanted to know.

"Don't you ever look at TV?" she demanded. "The key will fall out. I mean first we have to slip a paper or thin flat board under the door. Then when the key falls on it, we pull it toward us. We get the key, unlock the door, and we're out."

We searched for paper or a piece of cardboard, but gave up in a couple of minutes. Even with the light of the small ceiling bulb we couldn't find what we needed.

It wouldn't have mattered even if we had been successful. The slit under the door was quite narrow. Actually, I don't think you could have gotten a fine breath under it. The search helped to occupy our minds for a little while, however.

We hadn't noticed that the storm was passing us by. Oh, it didn't simply go away. There were the usual final cracks and roars, but we could tell that the heavy rain had begun to subside.

I had rested a while, but now I whacked the door with my feet, pounded with my fists till I skinned my knuckles, even tried whamming the door with my shoulder. You want some advice? Save your shoulder. That hurt like crazy.

We didn't know it then, of course, but my mom and dad were wide awake now. Mrs. Motley had run over when the storm subsided and she kept her finger on the bell until my dad staggered down to open the door.

Mom was at the top of the steps, worried and frightened, as she called down to my dad, "What is it, Thor? What's wrong?

Later, Mom confessed that between the doorbell, the sound of Mrs. Motley's voice raised in excitement, and the sudden realization of our screams in the attic, she suddenly understood my aunt Mildred. She swore it would take her a year to recover.

Of course we didn't know any of this at the time. But you can imagine our great relief when we heard the key turn in the door. Mom and Dad and Mrs. Motley burst in, afraid of what they might find. When they saw us, whole and unhurt, Dad leaped to a conclusion.

"Nora Jean Adams," he began.

Before she could say anything, I leaped to her defense. "Wait a minute, Dad. Let me tell you what's happened up here."

"Can we talk downstairs in the kitchen?" Mrs. Motley pleaded. "I could use a cuppa. I've got a tale to tell you—" she stopped to shake her head—"I can hardly believe it myself."

It was great to be in the kitchen, with the

lights on, the kettle about to whistle, all of us seated around the table. It was comfortable, cozy, *safe*. Even the storm had moved off.

"Stop fussing and sit down," Dad instructed Mom. "All right, Harvey. Let's get to the bottom of this. What were you two doing up in the attic . . ."

Mrs. Motley interrupted. "I think you should hear me out first, love."

"Later, Mrs. Motley. All right, Harvey. We're waiting."

I went clear back to when I first heard footsteps in the attic. Of course, Nora didn't just sit by while I explained. After a while, we sounded like a noisy duet.

When I got to the part about the two prowlers, Mom drew in such a deep breath, I thought she'd never be able to exhale again.

"We could all have been murdered in our beds," Mrs. Motley exclaimed. Her voice was hollow, but her eyes glittered with excitement.

Dad glared at her. He didn't say anything, but you could almost hear the words he held

back. He doesn't like extravagant state-
ments.

Just the same, when Nora came to the
part about the hanging judge, he threw back
his head and roared with laughter. He sure
is full of surprises.

Before I could get a word in edgewise,
Nora announced, as if she had thought of it
all by herself, "They were the counterfeiters, Uncle Thor. Wally Wurble and Kookie
Smith. The short fat one and the long thin
one. They wanted that printing plate real
bad."

Mom sighed. "I can't believe any of this.
Thieves in our attic . . ."

"Counterfeiters, Mom," I corrected her.

She waved that aside. "Whatever, Harvey. How could they have known where that
miserable plate was in the first place?"

"I've heard enough," Dad said. "I'm calling Oaty Clark right now."

"At this hour in the morning? You can't
be serious," Mom said.

Mrs. Motley helped herself to her third
cuppa. Then she held up her hand for silence. "I think," she began, "before you

take any such action, love, you'd best be listening to my tale."

Dad sank back in his chair. He's not the most patient man in the world, but he is a very courteous person.

Mrs. Motley pushed her cuppa aside. Then she leaned forward, her glance darting from face to face.

And the story she told was strange. Or maybe weird is a better word.

11

In which a gruesome tale is told

"You know how I love storms," Mrs. Motley began.

Everyone nodded. The whole neighborhood knows about Mrs. Motley and storms. Give her black clouds roiling across the sky, thunder to split the earth beneath with sheer noise, lightning so jagged and sharp it cuts the clouds like a hot knife through butter— there's Mrs. Motley on her porch, comfortable in her rocker, a pot of tea on the table, ready for the big show.

Dad waited. He knew better than to try to hurry her. She loves to talk, and we were her captive audience.

"Well, there I was, and the storm was sort of readying up," she began, "when who do you think I saw?" She didn't wait for an answer, just hurried on. "That nurse person pushing poor old Mrs. Grandy in her wheelchair."

"My word," Mom interrupted. "Mrs. Grandy must have had insomnia the worst yet, to be out so late and with a storm threatening."

"Exactly what I thought, love. Well, I felt real sorry for the poor old soul, so when time passed and she and the nurse didn't come back, I was worried, don't you see?" She shook her head and sighed. "It never takes them that long to go around the block. So I thought I'd best take a look-see."

Dad stifled his impatience, especially after my mom sent him a warning glance.

"So I came down from the porch, thinking I'd walk up to the corner anyway, to see if I could spot them. And just as I passed by your house, my eye was caught by something jammed under your hedge. I thought I'd better see what it was . . ."

Dad looked up at the ceiling; Mom buried her smile in the palm of her hand. Mrs. Motley just happened to see something? She

just thought she ought to investigate it?
Mom says Mrs. Motley ought to be an un-
dercover agent. Nothing escapes her eagle
eye.

Nora couldn't wait to hear what that
something was. "What was it? What was it?"
she asked in exasperation.

"Mrs. Grandy's wheelchair. Empty!"

Nora gasped. I just stared at Mrs. Motley,
fascinated. Why would the nurse have hidden the wheelchair in our hedge? I knew
the spot where it must have been, a rather
large break where Dad had cut away some
rotten branches.

"Then I heard voices," Mrs. Motley went
on. She certainly had our full attention now.
"So I hid on the other side of the hedge.
And a good thing, too. Next thing I knew,
two men came racing out of your house."

Mom turned so pale I thought she was
about to pass out. Nora and I had already
told her about the prowlers in the attic. But
hearing it again chilled her. I knew exactly
how she felt. Having someone break into
your home, especially when you're asleep,
is real scary.

"Will you go on?" Dad asked. He looked very angry. "What happened then?"

"They were dressed head to toe all in black," Mrs. Motley went on. "With ski caps pulled down over their faces. And I heard them say, clear as a bell, 'Well, that puts an end to the nurse and Mrs. Grandy.' "

"But why?" Mom asked. "It makes no sense at all." She turned to Dad. "I think you'd better get Oaty."

"Just a minute, Joy." Dad leaned in closer to Mrs. Motley. "You couldn't have been mistaken? You actually heard those words?"

"I'd swear to it on a stack of Bibles," she told him. "And then I sneezed." Mrs. Motley's head went up and down.

"And they caught you." Nora jumped to the obvious conclusion.

"Oh no, love. I guess that scared them. They were acting pretty jumpy themselves. One of them said to the other 'I'm out of here,' and he took off as if a demon was nipping his heels. The other wasn't far behind, I can tell you."

This was better than some of the scary

shows on TV. "So did you go back to your house and call the police?" I asked.

Mrs. Motley shook her head. "To tell you the truth, I didn't think of it. I took the wheelchair and put it on my porch. To protect it," she added in a hurry. "And you know the basket that hangs on the handles in back of the chair?" She didn't wait for an answer. "It happened to be open. I mean the lid was up."

And I knew who put that lid up. With her curiosity, she wasn't able to resist. I knew that as if I had actually seen her lift the lid.

"And?" my dad prompted.

"Inside that basket . . ." Mrs. Motley stopped.

"Inside that basket," Nora said, about to burst with excitement.

"Inside that basket was a nurse's uniform and Mrs. Grandy's dress, along with two pairs of shoes." She stopped to take a long sip of tea. "And it's my opinion, Judge," she told my dad, "there has been foul play done this night. Foul play," she repeated with gusto. Then she added, "They probably hid the bodies in your attic."

"We didn't see any bodies," I whispered to Nora.

"Well, we didn't look for any, did we?" she whispered back.

"That does it," my mom said. "Get Oaty, Thor. Get him now."

I had been doing some fast thinking. I held out my hand and grabbed his arm. "Dad, wait. I think you should hear what I have to tell you first. It's important," I added, when he hesitated.

Dad sat down again.

"Whatever it is, tell it fast," he instructed me. "There's no time to be wasted now."

"I know who those men are. I can give you their names. I can even tell you where you can find them."

"You can?" Nora looked upset. "What do you know that I don't, Harvey?"

I gave her my best superior smile.

"You'll know in a minute, Nora," I said. "Everyone will know."

12

In which Harvey
solves the mystery

Now that I had everyone's attention, I
wasn't sure how to begin. With the footsteps
in the attic? After all, that was the way it
started. But I had already mentioned that.
Finally, I decided just to plunge right in any
old way.

"Those two guys wanted that printing
plate real bad," I said. "So of course they
had to be the counterfeiters. What I couldn't
figure out was how they knew the printing
plate was in our attic."

"They couldn't have known," Nora interrupted.

I ignored her. "Dad," I went on, "do you
remember when Buttons ran out of the
house, with the plate in his mouth?"

Dad nodded. Of course he remembered. I could tell by the way his expression grew grim.

"The nurse was there . . ."

"Harvey," Mom put in. "Can you just stick to the point without wandering all over the place? What's the nurse got to do with anything?"

Mrs. Motley put her hand on my mom's arm. "Let the boy tell this his own way, love."

I flashed her a grateful look.

"Do you know what she said, Dad?" I went on.

My dad frowned, then shook his head.

"She said that Buttons was up the tree, and he had the printing plate in his mouth."

"So what, Harvey?" Nora said. "We all knew that."

"Did we? How did *she* know what Buttons had in his mouth? No one had even mentioned it while she was in the kitchen."

Mom was puzzled. "Does that really matter, Harvey?"

"I didn't think anything about it myself.

Not then. But then I wondered. Those two guys . . . who told them where the printing plate was?"

"The nurse," Nora shouted. "She was in on it with them, wasn't she, Harvey?"

I didn't answer, just got to the next step in what I had figured out.

"That nurse was awfully anxious to help. Why? She'd kept strictly to herself. I mean, she wasn't especially friendly, and certainly not to Mom. Right, Mom?"

"Well, Harvey," Mom said. "It's not easy to care for a helpless invalid. I didn't expect her to be sociable."

"Right," I agreed. "So how come she suddenly wanted to be helpful? Why did she follow us up to the attic? What was her interest in whether we got the plate away from Buttons or not?"

"It's your story," Dad said. "Get on with it."

"She knew about the printing plate, and she was desperate to know if we found it in the attic, because . . ." I stopped, took a deep breath, then blurted out, "because she

never was a nurse at all. I mean she wasn't
a she. She was a he . . . Kookie Smith, one
of the counterfeiters."

Mrs. Motley stared at me as if I had just
solved the riddle of the universe. "Well, I
declare. All this time we were so sorry for
Mrs. Grandy, and all the while they were
thumbing their noses at us."

"So the other one . . . old Mrs.
Grandy . . . isn't Mrs. Grandy at all.
She's . . . he's really Wally Wurble," Nora
said. She beamed at me, as if she had known
this all along.

"So there are no bodies in your attic."
Mrs. Motley sounded almost disappointed.

"I don't understand," Mom said. "What
was the purpose of pretending to be a nurse
and an invalid? No one around here knew
Wally Wurble or Kookie Smith. Why
couldn't they just be who they really are?"

"Simple," Dad told her. "They wanted
to impress all the neighbors they were just
two harmless people. After a while, nobody
paid any attention to them at all."

"But Uncle Thor," Nora objected. "Why

couldn't they be around in the daytime and counterfeit at night?"

"They probably found it more comfortable to work during the day," I said. "Most people like to sleep at night," I added, as a reminder of the way she woke me at an unearthly hour.

"It doesn't make sense," my mom said. "If the two men were already clothed from head to toe in black, why take the wheelchair? And why leave the clothing they wore as women in the basket?"

I had a ready answer for that, too. "Sure it makes sense, Mom," I argued. "Or it did to them anyway. See, they leave the house as the nurse and Mrs. Grandy, right?"

I didn't wait for an answer. I was sure I had it all figured out. "It was dark, and threatening, what with the storm and all. But suppose—just suppose—somebody happened to be up and looking out the window. What would they do if they spotted two men all covered up like that? They'd call the police, that's what," I said.

"So they came out of their house dressed

the way they always did. Then they came
here, stripped out of those clothes, stashed
them in the basket, and hid the wheelchair
under the hedge," Nora chimed in, her eyes
wide with excitement.

"Right," I said. "Then they planned to
come out, put those clothes on again, and
just be poor old Mrs. Grandy and the nurse,
out for their usual walk."

"They didn't figure on me, love, did they
now?" Mrs. Motley laughed.

I beamed at her. "They didn't expect us
in the attic, either. Or to have a kid attack
them. And not finding the wheelchair really
did them in."

"And so they arranged it all, knowing everyone around here would leave them
strictly alone," Mrs. Motley marveled.
"Who would ever suspect anything was going on in that house?"

"If that's so," Mom wanted to know,
"how did Buttons get the plate?"

Nora shook her head, "Aunt Joy, don't
you know by now how clever Buttons is? He
can get in and out of the oddest places."

I sat back in my chair with a contented

sigh. "I guess I really solved the mystery,"
I said.

My dad got up then, patted me on the
shoulder, and went to call Oaty Clark.

"I'll tell you something else, Dad," I
called after him. "I'll bet by the time the
police get to Mrs. Grandy's house—I mean
the counterfeiters' house—they'll be long
gone."

I can't foresee the future, read tarot cards,
or peer into a crystal ball. But anyone, even
somebody with a pea-sized brain, could pre-
dict that Wally Wurble and Kookie Smith
would skedaddle. That's Mrs. Motley's
word. I like it, because it was exactly what
they did. By the time the police surrounded
the house, it was empty. Wally Wurble and
Kookie Smith were long gone. All they left
behind was the wheelchair, plus the clothing
they wore as women.

I thought Oaty Clark would be mad as a
hornet that they had escaped. But when I
asked him he didn't seem the least bit
upset.

"Harvey," he said, and shrugged.
"Sooner or later, we'll put our hands on

those two. They always slip up, one way or another."

Mrs. Motley hadn't budged from our house. In fact, she had brewed a whole new pot of tea and managed to drink it all before she finally got up to leave. "My," she said, as she opened the door to go home. "It's lovely when all the loose ends are tied up." She was almost out the door when she turned back to ask one more question.

"Speaking of loose ends, my dear," she said to Nora, "what are you going to do about Buttons?"

Nora didn't answer; she just stared at Mrs. Motley, tears welling in her eyes.

13

In which
Nora has the last word

"I've been thinking about it," Nora said. "And there's only one thing to do."

Her voice was so low, we could hardly hear her. She swallowed a few times before she could go on. "Buttons must have been somebody's pet. You can tell from the way he feels so comfortable with people."

"And from the way he opens the refrigerator door," I chimed in. "And turns on television sets."

Nora grinned suddenly. "He's so smart."

My dad nodded. "What's the one thing we have to do?" he asked Nora.

"Advertise. Say we've found a pet raccoon. Somebody out there must be miserable because Buttons—" she paused, "or whatever he was called before, is here."

Mom got up and hugged Nora. "I'm very proud of you, Nora. You've just made a very difficult decision."

So that's what we did—advertised in the lost and found column. Nora and I also made up posters which we put up in some stores, and nailed to some trees. Several days went by, and no one showed up. Nora, who had begun with a gloomy face and dragging spirits, began to perk up considerably. Then one morning, the doorbell rang. When my mom opened the door, a girl of about nine or so stood there with her dad.

Before anyone had a chance to speak, the girl spotted Buttons in Nora's arms.

Her face glowed with joy. "Pumpernickel," she cried.

Buttons leaped out of Nora's arms and made a beeline for the girl at the door.

"Pumpernickel," the girl said again. If I could have bottled the light in her eyes, I could have made a fortune selling it as liquid sunshine. Buttons settled in her arms as if he had come home.

"She called him *Pumpernickel*," Nora whispered to me in disbelief. "What kind of name is that for a raccoon?"

I didn't think it was any worse than the name Buttons, but I remained silent.

While Nora gave Buttons one last hug, I had an idea. "Can you wait one more minute?" I asked the girl's father, when he said they had to leave. When he nodded, I raced upstairs to Georgeann's room and got the brass buckle I had returned, and flew down the steps again.

"Here," I said to Buttons.

The little girl was startled. "What is it?" she asked.

"It's something for Buttons—I mean Pumpernickel—to remember us by. Especially Nora."

"Harvey," Nora said. "What about Georgeann? She'll kill you."

"I'll make it up to her somehow," I said. Even if I couldn't, I thought maybe she'd understand. Maybe I could even ask Hank Clay where I could buy another buckle just like it. That way Georgeann would never know.

When they left, Buttons was cuddled in the little girl's arms, but he held fast to that buckle. Then Nora surprised me. She kissed me on the cheek. She actually kissed me. Of course I rubbed it off right away. I hate that kind of mushy stuff.

"You want to play Monopoly?" I asked. We went into the living room. While I set up the game, I looked up to find Nora studying me.

"I'll tell you what, Harvey," she said. "Instead of me coming here for Christmas vacation, why don't you come to my house?"

Losing Buttons must have affected her mind. Me? Get on a plane? *Fly?* I don't have Nora's imagination. She probably dreams that she's on the back of an eagle. I wouldn't mind flying except for three things: when the plane takes off, when it's in the air, and when it lands.

"Why would I want to come to your house?" I wondered. I didn't add "and get on a plane and have Aunt Mildred waiting at the other end?" I'd be a nervous wreck in sixty seconds flat.

She studied me for a couple of minutes

before she said, "I'm trying to talk my dad into starting an ostrich farm."

I was thunderstruck. I could feel an hysterical giggle work its way up into my throat.

An *ostrich* farm?

"Nora," I told her, "that isn't even a real bird. It can't fly. It's silly looking. It's big. It's awkward. It's . . ." I ran out of words.

"It's clever, and adorable, and huggable." Nora's voice had frost in it.

Huggable? I closed my eyes and tried to picture Nora hugging an ostrich. Go on. Close your eyes. Can you imagine it?

I thought not.

"Nora," I told her. "It would be the one and only thing that would get me on a plane, the chance to see you with your arms around an ostrich."

There were still a few more days left for her stay. She never mentioned ostriches in that time, so I took it for granted she had dropped the whole wild idea. But when we took her to the airport, she said, just before she left us to get on the plane, "I'll see you Christmastime."

As usual, Nora had the last word.

As we left the airport, I was lost in thought. Was it possible Nora could talk her dad into starting an ostrich farm? What would my aunt Mildred's reaction be—after they scraped her off the ceiling, that is?

An ostrich farm!

I leave it up to you.

What do you think?